delight

30 DEVOTIONS
FOR FINDING JOY

LIFEWAY STUDENTS DEVOTIONS

© 2020 LifeWay Press®

No part of this work may be reproduced or transmitted in any form or by any means, electronic or mechanical, including photocopying and recording, or by any information storage or retrieval system, except as may be expressly permitted in writing by the publisher. Requests for permission should be addressed in writing to LifeWay Press®, One LifeWay Plaza, Nashville, TN 37234.

ISBN 978-1-0877-4092-8
Item 005831347
Dewey Decimal Classification Number: 242
Subject Heading: DEVOTIONAL LITERATURE / BIBLE STUDY AND TEACHING / GOD

Printed in the United States of America

Student Ministry Publishing
LifeWay Resources
One LifeWay Plaza
Nashville, Tennessee 37234

We believe that the Bible has God for its author; salvation for its end; and truth, without any mixture of error, for its matter and that all Scripture is totally true and trustworthy. To review LifeWay's doctrinal guideline, please visit www.lifeway.com/doctrinalguideline.

Unless otherwise noted, all Scripture quotations are taken from the Christian Standard Bible®, Copyright © 2017 by Holman Bible Publishers. Used by permission. Christian Standard Bible® and CSB® are federally registered trademarks of Holman Bible Publishers.

publishing team

Director, Student Ministry
Ben Trueblood

Manager, Student Ministry Publishing
John Paul Basham

Editorial Team Leader
Karen Daniel

Content Editor
Kyle Wiltshire

Production Editor
Stephanie Cross

Graphic Designer
Kaitlin Redmond

table of contents

04 Intro

05 Getting Started

06 Where does joy come from?

18 What does real joy look like?

30 Why do people get depressed?

40 How should Christians respond to depression?

50 How can real joy overcome depression?

64 What do you do when being joyful is hard?

intro

If you went to an amusement park for a day you'd probably have a lot of fun. The next day you might remember the fun you had and it would make you smile, but it wouldn't be the same as being there. A few weeks later the smile that day brought you might fade. Eventually, you might forget about the day entirely. What was fun for a moment, didn't last; it didn't bring you real, sustaining joy.

Joy is something many people don't understand and, quite honestly, struggle with. Some believe joy means fun, but they are two different things. Joy doesn't fade or diminish over time. You can experience joy in good times and bad. Joy is not rooted in your circumstances or situation. Other people, their opinion of you, or your relationship to them can't dictate whether or not you have joy. Joy—real, lasting, joy—comes from somewhere else entirely.

We all want to know what real, lasting joy is and where to find it; how to experience it; and how we can help others be joyful too.

Over the next 30 days, we will explore what the Bible says about joy. We will dig into the opposite of joy—depression—and see why it affects so many people. We will also point to key truths that help us see how to cultivate fulfilling and enduring joy.

God's Word speaks clearly on this matter. So, let's dive in and see what He says about joy and how we can experience it.

getting started

This devotional contains 30 days of content, divided into sections that each answer a specific question related to joy. Each day is broken down into three elements—discover, delight, and display—to help you answer core questions related to Scripture.

discover | This section helps you examine the passage in light of who God is and determine what it says about your identity in relationship to Him. Included here is the key passage and focus Scripture, along with illustrations and commentary to guide you as you study.

delight | In this section, you'll be challenged by questions and activities that help you see how God is alive and active in every detail of His Word and your life. You'll be guided to ask yourself what the passage means when it comes to your relationship with God.

display | Here's where you really take action. Display calls you to apply what you've learned from each day's study.

prayer | Each day also includes a prayer activity in one of the three main sections.

Throughout the devotional, you'll also find extra articles and activities to help you connect with the topic personally, such as Scripture memory verses, articles, and a list of resources.

Section 1: WHERE DOES JOY COME FROM?

day 1

FIRST THINGS FIRST

discover

> At the start of this journey of learning to delight and find joy, spend some time in prayer. Ask God to reveal to you what true joy is.

It's easy to see that we live in a fallen, sinful world. Sickness, suffering, and sorrow surround us. Sometimes, life becomes so difficult that it's hard to find joy. These feelings can lead us to despair; to think our lives have no meaning. As Christians, it's even tempting to consider this life as something we just have to get through until we get to spend eternity with Jesus. But Jesus made it clear that God intended for us to do more than just exist.

READ
MATTHEW 6:33.

"But seek first the kingdom of God and his righteousness, and all these things will be provided for you."

This comes from a section of Jesus' teaching on worry. He was instructing His listeners not to spend their lives focused on things of lesser concern, like food and clothing. Instead, Jesus taught them—and us—to focus on God first and to live life His way. When we seek God first, everything else falls into the right order. That is the first step to finding joy.

delight |

What did Jesus have to say about the purpose of our lives? Write it in your own words.

How do you seek God's kingdom first in your daily routine and activities?

How have you experienced joy by seeking God first in your life?

display |

Nothing God creates is meaningless. He created humanity on purpose, with purpose. Believers' lives should be focused on growing in our relationship with Him and building His kingdom on Earth. As we do this, our joy increases.

> Think about your family, church, school, community, teams, clubs, and your group of friends. Where has God placed you? How can you model joy with these people in your life? How can you live focused on His purpose with these people? List at least two ideas you'll put into practice this week.

Are there situations in your life that feel pointless? Do you wonder how God could ever use them for His glory? Be honest with God about those circumstances today. Ask Him to open your eyes to how He is at work. Ask Him to give you joy in spite of the hardships you face.

Use page 16 to help you memorize today's focus verse.

day 2

BELIEVING IS SEEING

discover

If joy begins with putting God first, then what sustains it? Even when we try to make God our top priority and live for His kingdom, sorrow and sin remain active in the world. It's important for us to know how to persist in finding joy.

READ
1 PETER 1:8-9.

Though you have not seen him, you love him; though not seeing him now, you believe in him, and you rejoice with inexpressible and glorious joy, because you are receiving the goal of your faith, the salvation of your souls.

In these verses, Peter was teaching about true faith, describing the very essence of faith in verse 8: Even though we have never seen God with our eyes, we love and believe in Him. Because of the work of Jesus' death on the cross and resurrection from the grave, we can have life now and in eternity. The result of this reality in our lives is, as Peter put it, "inexpressible and glorious joy" (v. 8).

Simply put: it is impossible to sustain joy in our lives without faith.

delight |

How do we know God is real and active in our lives, even though we have never seen Him?

How has your faith helped you remain joyful?

> As you continue to focus on where joy comes from, take a moment to thank God for giving you faith. Ask Him to increase your faith when life becomes difficult. Consider writing out your prayer here.

display |

Joy is nourished by faith. It's not easy to remain rooted in faith, but as we do, we'll find our joy increasing. We remain rooted in our faith when we seek God's kingdom and His righteousness first.

The word nourish means to nurture, sustain, or grow. Grab three sticky notes or index cards. On separate index cards, write out a few ways you can do the following: nurture your joy, sustain your joy, and grow your joy. Look up the individual words to guide you if needed.

day 3

CERTAIN HOPE

discover

Basketball legend Michael Jordan once said, "I've missed more than 9,000 shots in my career. I've lost almost 300 games. Twenty-six times I've been trusted to take the game-winning shot and missed. I've failed over and over and over again in my life. And that is why I succeed."[1] In spite of this quote, no one would claim Michael Jordan was a failure. But, as talented as he was, his success was never a certainty. Now, imagine someone whose success was guaranteed.

READ
ROMANS 15:7-13.

Now may the God of hope fill you with all joy and peace as you believe so that you may overflow with hope by the power of the Holy Spirit. —Romans 15:13

The hope described here is not the same as the desire for something to turn out the way we want—like our favorite player hitting the game winning basket. Our hope in God is not based on chance or strong desires, but on certainty. We know this because of Jesus' life, death, burial, and resurrection. God permanently secured our hope through Jesus.

This hope is not something that may or may not come through for us—God will always come through. God doesn't always work things out the way we want Him to, but things always happen just as He intends.

Hope from God is the source of overflowing joy for those who believe. As we put Him first and see His faithfulness, our relationship with God grows—and our faith and joy grow too.

delight |

There are many ways to grow in your relationship with God. What you are doing right now is one of them. Reading His Word, thinking deeply about it, and focusing your heart and mind on His truth are great ways to grow in your relationship with Him.

Name one way you've grown in your relationship with God in the last year.

How have you seen your joy increase as you've grown closer to God?

How have you seen God come through for you when you've needed Him?

display |

God often uses others to help us when we're going through something difficult.

Write down the name of a person who God used to help you when you were in need. Take a moment to text or call that person. Let them know how God used them to help you.

> **Finding joy in your relationship with God requires you to be actively seeking Him. Spend some time in prayer, asking God to give you a continued desire to know Him more.**

day 4

MADE TO WORSHIP

discover

Who in your life brightens up your day? Who brings you joy when you're around them? Maybe you love being around them because they are funny, kind, or encouraging. Regardless of why you enjoy being with them, focus for a second on the feeling you have when you're in that person's presence. Spending time with God can bring you an even greater joy than being with this person.

READ
PSALM 16.

You reveal the path of life to me; in your presence is abundant joy; at your right hand are eternal pleasures. —Psalm 16:11

In today's passage, David—the author of Psalm 16—revealed his feelings toward God saying, "I have nothing good besides you" (v. 2), "Lord, you are my ... cup of blessing" (v. 5), and "I will always let the Lord guide me"(v. 8). These phrases indicate that spending time with God brought the deepest joy in David's life.

God's presence gives "abundant joy" (v. 11). Worship is one of the best ways to experience this type of closeness with God. You can worship God corporately when you gather with other believers. But worshiping God on your own is important too, when it's just you and God, and no one can see you. It's necessary to your spiritual health to experience both types of worship in your life.

delight

We were made to worship. Anything we allow to consume our hearts and minds can be an object of worship. Sometimes we misdirect our worship to other things like sports, school, social media, and so on.

Think about where you may be directing your worship. How can you redirect your worship toward God?

Have you ever experienced the joy in worship David described? Explain.

display

Take a minute to worship God. Use a streaming service or search for a worship song in your personal music library that speaks to your heart and play it. Close your eyes, sing along, focus on the words, kneel, or lift your hands. Do whatever you feel led to do. No one is watching. Worship God and experience the joy of the Lord.

> Write out the word *worship*. Use it to create an acrostic that describes how you feel about the Lord. Let these words serve as a time of joyful prayer to God for all He's done for you.

day 5

CHOOSING JOY

discover

READ
PSALM 118.

*This is the day the L*ORD *has made; let's rejoice and be glad in it.*
—Psalm 118:24

This Psalm describes a king's victorious return after battle. The psalmist made it clear that God won the battle—but the victory wasn't easy for them. He wrote about being in distress (v. 5), being hated (v. 7), surrounded (v. 10), and pushed (v. 13). In verse 18, he even talked about how severely the Lord disciplined him.

In spite of all of this, his praise in verse 24 is one of the most well known: "This is the day the Lord has made, let's rejoice and be glad in it!" In spite of being distressed, hated, surrounded by his enemies, pushed and disciplined by God—the psalmist still chose to delight in the Lord.

So far, we have learned that joy comes from seeking God first, and is nourished by faith, continued through our relationship with God, and enriched by worship. Today, we learn a new and necessary truth: Joy is a choice. Like the psalmist, we must choose to have joy, even in tough times.

> **Take a minute to pray right now. Ask God to help you choose joy, no matter what circumstances you face. Write out your prayer in a journal or on a blank piece of paper.**

LifeWay Students | Devotions

delight |

While we don't have to like what we're going through, we can still rejoice. Why? Because what we believe to be true about God will determine if we can choose joy, even in the middle of difficulties and trials.

List five things you believe to be true about God. Search through your Bible to find out if what you believe about Him is true. (*Hint: Psalm 118 is a good place to begin your search.*)

Reflect on a circumstance you endured where God ultimately gave you victory. How did He sustain you through the trial? How did He give you joy in spite of the difficulty?

display |

Post Psalm 118:24 on whatever social media platform you use. If anyone comments, choose joy as you respond. If you don't use social media, write it out on a sticky note and put it on your bathroom mirror.

If you are walking through a difficult time, go back to the prayer you just wrote. Keep it in a place where you won't forget it and return to it whenever you need to choose joy. Ask God for help when you need it.

MEMORY VERSE

"But seek first the kingdom of God and his righteousness,

and all these things will be provided for you."

MATTHEW 6:33

day 6

INTO THE UNKNOWN

discover

If you've ever wondered when you'd figure out everything in your life, then you're not alone. No one has it all figured out. So, what do we do as we try to understand what our lives should look like?

READ
JOSHUA 1:6-9.

"Haven't I commanded you: be strong and courageous? Do not be afraid or discouraged, for the LORD your God is with you wherever you go." —Joshua 1:9

For 40 years, Moses led the Hebrews as they wandered in the wilderness on the edge of the promised land. When Moses died, the burden of leading the people fell to Joshua. In today's passage, God was encouraging Joshua and building him up for the task of conquering the land He'd promised to them. Talk about not having it all figured out. All Joshua had to go on was what God told him—and that was enough.

Sometimes we feel like we'll only experience joy when we know the whole picture. Joshua didn't know exactly what would happen as they entered the promised land, but he knew God was with him. He knew God had given them His law (the Ten Commandments) to follow. And he knew they would have success if he stayed on the path God had placed before him.

delight

Real joy is not knowing everything that's in front of us; it's knowing God is with us as we go.

What "unknown" are you facing right now? How do God's words to Joshua give you hope?

Think about difficult situations you've faced in the past. Did your worry about the outcome dominate your thoughts? How did God walk with you through that time?

> Life isn't like a movie or book where our circumstances neatly resolve before the credits roll. However, knowing God is with us makes a difference. Pray that you would be sensitive to God's presence with you as you navigate whatever difficulties you may be facing.

display

We experience joy in the unknown when we experience God. If we try to walk through the difficult days without Him, we won't experience joy along the way.

God took around 600 years to bring the Hebrews into the promised land. Just because you don't have what He's promised you today doesn't mean you never will. Instead of focusing on what you don't have, focus on what God has given you. Rejoice in that and write down three things He's done for you.

Seek out someone who is having a tough day. Just sit with them. You don't have to give them advice. Listen to them—maybe all they need is for someone to care.

day 7

FINISH THE RACE

discover

Have you ever run an endurance race, like a 5K or even a marathon? If you have, you know how much work it takes to prepare for this type of event. Although many people compete in endurance races, not all runners enter the race to win. For some, it's more about the accomplishment, about pushing themselves toward greater endurance and rejoicing in the work they put in just to cross the finish line. It's about the growth and the journey.

READ
JAMES 1:2-4.

Consider it a great joy, my brothers and sisters, whenever you experience various trials, because you know that the testing of your faith produces endurance. And let endurance have its full effect, so that you may be mature and complete, lacking nothing.

The truth is finding joy is like an endurance race. All Christians will experience trying times throughout life, but just like training for a long distance race we have to keep pressing forward. Christians must remember that trials are like the months of preparation that will get us across the finish line.

Trials are never easy, but we ultimately know that Jesus helps us become mature and complete in all things. As we grow in faith, we learn that there can even be joy in the trials.

delight

Think about something you had to work hard to achieve. Whether it was for a project in school, an athletic event, or even something you made with your hands. What made all the hard work worth it?

Apply that same understanding to your faith. Spending time with God in worship, study of His Word, and prayer (among other things), brings us joy and helps us through those difficult circumstances. Reflect on a difficult season God brought you through, writing about it in a journal or notebook.

display

Even if you're a Christian, you might be thinking: "I just can't imagine joy at the end of what I'm going through." It's okay. This is when your faith sustains you beyond your feelings.

Read Psalm 118:24. Now, consider this: *Joy is a choice*. We don't have to delight in our trials, but we delight in the God who is greater than our hardships.

Sometimes God allows us to experience a trial because it will help someone else who is walking through the same thing. Think about those around you. Ask God to reveal anyone around you who might benefit from hearing about your experience. Write out their names and commit to sharing your story with them this week. Remember, the point is not to tell how *you* overcame, but to point them to God and how He helped you overcome.

> **Pray a bold prayer today. Ask God to use the trials you endure to make you mature and complete so that you will lack nothing.**

day 8

INSIDE OUT

discover

The early church faced a controversial question: What was right for a believer to eat? This may not seem like a big deal to you, but this question was rooted in the Jewish beliefs still held by many of the first Christians. Jews had very specific laws about their diet, so when they became Christians, they had a tough time walking away from their old ways of thinking. They needed to learn that joy was not found in judging what their fellow believers did or didn't eat. Real joy came from somewhere else.

READ
ROMANS 14:13-23.

Therefore, do not let your good be slandered, for the kingdom of God is not eating and drinking, but righteousness, peace, and joy in the Holy Spirit. Whoever serves Christ in this way is acceptable to God and receives human approval.
—Romans 14:16-18

This type of thinking still exists in churches today, but it looks different. Instead of judging someone for what they do or don't eat, believers might criticize others for how they look or because they hold a different opinion from our own. Truthfully, it's difficult not to live in this space, but we'll never find joy living in judgment.

Jesus didn't build His church on appearances; He built His church on what happens on the inside, in our hearts. The Holy Spirit is the One who helps shape us and mold us in righteousness, peace, and joy. So, real joy doesn't come from looking the part on the outside, but by letting the Lord change us from the inside out.

It's so tempting to just try to look the part, but that won't last. Eventually what's really on the inside will emerge and become evident to those around us.

> **Ask God to shape you from the inside out and to keep you from not judging others by their outward appearance.**

delight

To be changed on the inside, we must look at our own hearts and ask ourselves some tough questions. Take a few minutes and ask yourself:

Where have I been guilty of judging others and thinking it will make me feel good about myself?

What attitudes need to change in my own heart so that I can experience the righteousness, peace, and joy described in verse 17?

display

When we seek to be changed from within by the Holy Spirit, we gain the approval of both God and people (v. 18). This means our motives are revealed to be pure in all that we do. Does this describe you? Why or why not?

Examine your heart and see if the good you seek to do is from a pure motive. If it's not, confess to God and repent of any impure motives.

Do something good for someone else quietly, without taking credit for the deed. Pray that God would give you more opportunities to love others well without any thought of personal gain.

day 9

ONCE LOST

discover

Think back to a time when you got a good grade on a test or project. Remember how good it felt to show your parents the grade or casually mention your score to your friends (getting your humblebrag on)? Even thinking back on the experience might make you feel good inside but the initial rush wears off over time. Ultimately, the good feeling of the moment does not amount to real, lasting joy.

READ
LUKE 15:8-10.

"I tell you, in the same way, there is joy in the presence of God's angels over one sinner who repents." —Luke 15:10

In this parable, the coin the woman lost was worth about what someone would get paid for a day of work.[2] This wasn't overkill; it wasn't like turning the house over for a penny. Her diligence to find it revealed she wasn't a person of great means. She needed that coin to live, so when she found the coin, she wanted to tell everyone she knew.

The point of the parable is that each person is of infinite value and worth to God. When someone comes to faith in Jesus, it's not just a passing thing that wears off over time. It means someone has moved from death to life. This lasting celebration is what real joy looks like.

> **For today, the Delight section of the devotion will be an extended time of prayer. Take a minute to prepare your heart to spend some time in an attitude and posture of prayer.**

delight |

Do you understand just how valuable you are to God? He loves you so much that He sent His only Son to die for you. Take a moment and reflect on that.

Thank Jesus that He willingly gave His life so that you could live.

Who were the people in your life that diligently poured into you, witnessed to you, and loved you until you God rescued you? Thank God for those people and their desire to see you come to faith in Christ.

display |

Pure joy comes when someone repents of sin and turns to Christ—that is lasting, sustaining joy.

Who are the lost people in your life? Think about the joy you would feel if they came to faith in Jesus. Think about the eternal joy they would feel giving their lives to Christ. What can you do to plant or water a seed of faith for them?

This devotional has consistently pointed to the truth that true joy is found in Jesus. Is that evident by the life you lead? What can do that reveals this truth in your life? How can you make this joy more evident to those around you?

Delight

day 10

WHAT WILL YOU CHOOSE?

discover

Some people talk about their lives as if everything is already determined and there is nothing anyone can do to change it. What a joyless way to live. But the truth is, all people will experience the same outcome. Unless the Lord returns first, everyone will die. But, what we do with our lives isn't set in stone. We have a choice to make the most of it for God's glory.

READ
ECCLESIASTES 9:1-6.

But there is hope for whoever is joined with all the living, since a live dog is better than a dead lion. For the living know that they will die, but the dead don't know anything. There is no longer a reward for them because the memory of them is forgotten. —Ecclesiastes 9:4-5

Simply put: When you're alive, you have a choice in how you live; you don't when you're dead. A lion might be mightier and more majestic than a dog, but a live dog is better than a dead lion. Those of us who are Christians know we won't live here forever—when our time has come, we will be with the Lord. In the meantime, we must live for Him, seeking His kingdom and righteousness first.

However, those who do not believe don't realize that this life is their only chance. When it's over, they won't have another opportunity to make a different choice about how they live. At that point their choice will have been made.

delight

This truth can lead you two respond in two ways: You may feel sad or depressed because people who don't know the Lord can't experience the joy He has for them here and in eternity. Or you may be inspired by the truth to share this good news and joy with those around you.

Understanding that our time on earth is limited, take an inventory of your life. How are you spending your time? Are you giving your life to things that matter in eternity or to things that will fade away?

> **Talk to God about how you are spending your life. If you are not using it for Him and His glory, repent of that and ask God to help you turn in a new direction. If you are spending your days wisely, then thank God for the path He has you on and pray that He helps you stay on it.**

display

This ends the section on *What Real Joy Looks Like*. Consider the last five days of devotions as you respond to the following:

Jot down one new insight you had about what real joy looks like.

Are you seeking and choosing joy? Or are you mired in despair? If you're feeling down, ask God to shine a light to help you see how to escape despair.

how blue are you?

Everyone feels a little blue. But how do you know when you've moved from feeling down to outright depression? While this page is not meant to act as a diagnostic test, you'll find some questions to help you determine your level of depression. Use a blue highlighter to select the answer that best describes you.

1 I feel hopeless about pretty much everything.
Nope.   Eh, maybe.   Sometimes.   Definitely.

2 I'm tired most of the time, but I don't know why.
Nope.   Eh, maybe.   Sometimes.   Definitely.

3 I have felt really down; not even things or people I love can cheer me up.
Nope.   Eh, maybe.   Sometimes.   Definitely.

4 I haven't really wanted to do anything. Moving takes too much effort.
Nope.   Eh, maybe.   Sometimes.   Definitely.

5 I don't fall asleep easily, and I don't sleep well once I do.
Nope.   Eh, maybe.   Sometimes.   Definitely.

6 Most of the time, I want to stay in bed all day and do nothing.
Nope.   Eh, maybe.   Sometimes.   Definitely.

7 I struggle to feel joyful.
Nope.   Eh, maybe.   Sometimes.   Definitely.

8 I'm incredibly indecisive.
Nope.   Eh, maybe.   Sometimes.   Definitely.

9 I'm usually upset and can't sit still.
Nope.   Eh, maybe.   Sometimes.   Definitely.

10 At times, I've wondered if life is worth living.
Nope.   Eh, maybe.   Sometimes.   Definitely.

Every "Eh, maybe" answer is worth 1 point. Every "Sometimes" answer is worth 3 points, and every "Definitely" highlighted is worth 5 points. Total: _____.

These numbers indicate what your depression level is *likely* to be. 0-15 is low, 16-30 is moderate, and 31-50 is high. If you're feeling depressed at all, it would be a good idea to talk with your parents about meeting with your pastor, a certified Christian counselor, or your doctor for a personalized and professional assessment.[5]

what can i do when i'm feeling down?

While those who struggle with depression should seek professional help, here are some practical tips to add a little joy to your day when you're feeling down.

1. **Spend time with the people you love.** Sometimes, we just need someone to be there, to listen, or inspire us to move when we're down.

2. **Take care of yourself.** Getting enough sleep, eating foods that are good for you, drinking enough water, and exercising also help boost your mood.

3. **Get outside.** Maybe you're an avid hiker or dirt-bike rider, or maybe you enjoy walking through the city, looking at the architecture or maybe you'd rather watch the sun set over the lake. Spending time outside is good for your brain and your body.

4. **Counter every lie with a positive truth.** We all have certain lies we believe about ourselves, but God's Word is filled with the truth. And when we can't see our way to the light, family and friends can be a huge help! For every lie or negative thought that pops into your head, write out a truth. Consider keeping a journal specifically for this purpose.

5. **Laugh.** Right now, you may feel down, but you will experience joy again (Ps. 30:5). Watch a funny movie, TV show, or video online. You could also consider finding videos of a comedian like Tim Hawkins, Chonda Pierce, or Michael Jr.

6. **Get creative.** If you enjoy painting, singing, drawing, building things, graphic design, working on cars, photography, or any other creative activity, make time to do it.

What are some other ways you can create space for joy in your life?

This is neither an exhaustive list or therapeutic advice. For specific help in your own struggle, talk with a mental health professional.

day 11

SOMETHING'S NOT RIGHT

discover|

A recent study showed that 13 percent of all American teens have suffered from depression within the last year. Most of those surveyed identified depression and anxiety as a problem for their age group in their communities.[3] Depression is a common issue for countless people, but God can help us fight it.

READ
ROMANS 8:22-25.

For we know that the whole creation has been groaning together with labor pains until now. Not only that, but we ourselves who have the Spirit as the firstfruits—we also groan within ourselves, eagerly waiting for adoption, the redemption of our bodies.
—Romans 8:22-23

The word *groaning* points to an internal, inaudible prayer, typically filled with grief.[4] All of creation cries out with this grief because it is rooted in sin. When sin entered the world (Gen. 3), God's perfect design was distorted from its original intent. As a result, things like sickness, natural disasters, and suffering of all sorts—including depression—became a part of life on earth. But the greatest consequence of sin is death.

Depression isn't always a punishment from God because of our sin. Sometimes our personal sin does cause depression (we'll deal with that on Day 14), but depression is not always a result of sins we've committed. Depression can be biological, circumstantial, or even genetic. No matter what the cause of depression, it's important to understand this key truth: Depression exists because sin exists.

delight

Depression occurs because sin has tainted God's perfect creation. If there was no sin, then there would be no depression.

If you're suffering from depression, take a moment right now and recognize that it does not come from God. God loves us and does not want us to be depressed.

> We know God loves us and doesn't want us to be depressed, but wants us to be filled with joy. We can be confident of this truth because He sent Jesus to die for us. Take a moment and dwell on that truth. We have a chance at life because of Jesus.

display

Depression is a reality for many people today, even Christians; it doesn't magically go away just because you're a Christian. As verse 23 reminds us, even those of us with the Spirit "groan inwardly." But, we also know God offers hope.

If you are struggling with depression, find help. At minimum talk to a trusted adult—your parents, your youth pastor, or a mentor. If you need to talk to a professional counselor or therapist, please pursue that option. Don't let yourself struggle with depression alone. Take a look at the Resources on pages 48-49 for more information.

List three steps you will take to help you get through this difficult season.

If you don't struggle with depression, chances are you know someone who does. How might your attitude about depression need to change? How can you make yourself more available to walk with someone through it?

day 12

ONE STEP AT A TIME

discover

So much of what we find on the news or even on social media can be classified as bad news. It's no secret that we are surrounded by terrible things all the time. What we see on the news or online is on a broad scale, but it doesn't even speak to the difficult things we go through on a personal level. No wonder so many of us feel depressed and struggle to find joy.

READ
PSALM 94.

If I say, "My foot is slipping," your faithful love will support me, LORD. When I am filled with cares, your comfort brings me joy. —Psalm 94:18-19

The psalmist was no stranger to tragedy. This psalm speaks of wicked people who killed widows, foreigners, and orphans (v. 6). What can be done in the face of such evil? The overwhelming oppression caused the people to ask: Where is God? But the psalmist reminded them that God will never leave His people— and we can take comfort in this truth too (v. 14). Even when we are filled with worry, anxiety, or depression, God's love brings us joy.

Here's the truth: Some people are depressed because they've experienced awful things. Focusing on God's love won't automatically cure depression and give joy, but it trains your mind to focus on the good that comes from the Lord. Focusing on all that's gone wrong only leads to stronger negative thought patterns. So, one step toward joy is to look to God's love and not to dwell on the tragedies of life.

LifeWay Students | Devotions

delight |

Just as runners complete a marathon one step at a time, this is how we keep joy—one choice at a time. Choosing joy does not minimize tragedies you may have experienced. But, by choosing to focus on God's love, you can take the first step away from depression and toward joy.

What can you do to turn your attention from the tragedies you may have faced in life toward God's love and the joy He can provide?

display |

We can't ignore the fact that difficult circumstances can contribute to depression. You might even know someone who's dealing with something difficult, causing them to feel discouraged or depressed.

If you know someone in this situation, write their name on an index card or sticky note. Place the note in your Bible. Then, whenever you come across that name, pause and pray for them.

> **Focus your attention on God and His love. As a prayer exercise, write out anything about God's love that comes to mind. If you need more room to write, grab a sheet of paper or notebook. Then pray back through that list, thanking God for His love and letting that lead your thoughts.**

day 13

A REAL ENEMY

discover

READ
1 PETER 5:6-9.

Humble yourselves, therefore, under the mighty hand of God, so that he may exalt you at the proper time, casting all your cares on him, because he cares about you. —1 Peter 5:6-7

Some people struggle with depression because our enemy, Satan, is willing to do anything to keep them stuck there. His objective is to devour. He wants to rip away joy and make life miserable. Like a lion, he stalks and then attempts to consume his prey. Peter offers four ways we can offset the attacks of the enemy:

- Humble yourselves (v. 6).
- Cast your cares on God (v. 7).
- Be sober-minded and alert (v. 8).
- Resist (v. 9).

Highlight the phrase "throughout the world" (v. 9). Satan attacks every believer around the world. Be encouraged by the fact that you are not alone; you fight against the enemy alongside your brothers and sisters in Christ, and we can help one another face the temptation to live in discouragement and depression.

It's also good to remember God cares for us (v. 7). God didn't set these four actions before us to make life more difficult. He did it so we can experience joy and escape from the enemy's schemes. We don't act out of obligation. We act because we need God desperately, and because He's proven His love to us over and over.

LifeWay Students | Devotions

delight

Think about these four actions. Name one way you can do each of them to delight in the Lord and embrace joy.

- Humble yourself:

- Cast your cares on God:

- Be sober-minded and alert:

- Resist:

> **Now go back over what you wrote and restate each one as a prayer. You can structure your prayer like this:** *Lord, help me to humble myself by...*

display

Our God is stronger than our enemy. The Spirit that lives in us is greater than the one who lives in the world (1 John 4:4).

Where have you been vulnerable to attacks from the enemy? How can you build up your defenses against him? List three ideas to help you live in joy rather than despair.

When do you tend to think you are alone in fighting the enemy's lies? Name two other believers who are walking with you and fighting alongside you against the enemy.

Delight

day 14

JOY RESTORED

---

discover

Take a minute to review some of the reasons people experience depression. People are depressed because sin has marred God's original design for the world and the people in it. Depression also exists because people have truly terrible things happen to and around them. And depression comes because we have an enemy that wants to devour us and leave us in despair. But let's look at one more reason.

READ
PSALM 51:1-13.

God, create a clean heart for me and renew a steadfast spirit within me. Do not banish me from your presence or take your Holy Spirit from me. Restore the joy of your salvation to me, and sustain me by giving me a willing spirit.
—*Psalm 51:10-12*

In this Psalm, David sought forgiveness for adultery and murder. The prophet Nathan had confronted David with his sin, and David immediately felt conviction from the Lord. As a result of his sinful decisions, David slipped into a season of despair (v. 8). This psalm was David's prayer of repentance, where he asked God to deliver him from his sin.

Like David, our lack of joy in life is sometimes caused by our own sinfulness. Maybe a habit or a secret sin isolates us from God and others, and we feel alone and depressed because of it. But all of us have sinned, and the good news is, God offers forgiveness to all of us too. What we do once we realize we've sinned makes the difference between falling deeper into sadness or beginning the journey out of it.

delight |

David wanted to have a clean heart (v.10). For this to happen, he had to be willing to let God have complete control of his heart and his life.

Are you ready to let God have control of all of your heart? What has to happen in your life to give Him access to the "secret" places in your heart?

display |

Once God restored David and put him on the right path, David still had to live with the consequences of his choices. This didn't mean David didn't have God's love and forgiveness. But forgiveness doesn't mean the consequences of our sins vanish.

If you've sinned against someone else and God has revealed this to you, what will you do to try to restore the broken relationship you've caused?

> **Sometimes confession is the first step toward joy. If the Holy Spirit has convicted you of sin in your life that you need to confess, take the time to do so now.**

MEMORY VERSE

The Lord is my shepherd;
I HAVE WHAT I NEED.

He lets me lie down in green pastures;
HE LEADS ME BESIDE QUIET WATERS.

He renews my life;
HE LEADS ME ALONG THE RIGHT PATHS FOR HIS NAME'S SAKE.

Even when I go through the darkest valley,
I FEAR NO DANGER, FOR YOU ARE WITH ME;

**your rod and your staff—
they comfort me.**
YOU PREPARE A TABLE
BEFORE ME IN THE
PRESENCE OF MY ENEMIES;

you anoint my head with oil;
MY CUP OVERFLOWS.

**Only goodness and faithful
love will pursue me
all the days of my life,**
AND I WILL DWELL IN THE
HOUSE OF THE LORD
AS LONG AS I LIVE.

PSALM 23

day 15

WITH ME

discover

Unfortunately, there is a stigma attached to mental health within Christian community. Often the perception is that someone who is depressed is not walking faithfully with God. While sin can sometimes be the source of depression, it isn't always. Sometimes circumstances, brain chemistry, and even someone else's sin toward us triggers depression in us.

READ
PSALM 23.

Even when I go through the darkest valley, I fear no danger, for you are with me; your rod and your staff—they comfort me. —Psalm 23:4

David—who had his fair share of dark, depressing days—wrote this psalm. Many of David's most difficult days were the result of someone else's actions. In verse 4, David wrote about going "through the darkest valley." This valley might have been when he was in physical danger or mental anguish, or it could have been the result of emotional trauma. Regardless, when David was in that "darkest valley," he knew that the Lord was still with him, protecting him like a shepherd protects his sheep.

That is the take away for us: depression is like a dark valley some of us may walk into. If you find yourself in that dark valley, know that God is there for you.

delight |

Psalm 23 is a picture of a shepherd (God) and His sheep (us). The job of a shepherd is to watch over sheep who are prone to wander into dangerous places. This is the nature of our relationship with God as well. He watches over us and protects us.

When have you been in a dark valley? What led you to that place?

God is there for you—no matter where you are. How have you or will you place your faith and trust in the Lord to comfort you and walk with you through any valley?

display |

One of the best protections for us as we walk through valleys is God's Word. Knowing Scripture can help you fend off attacks from the enemy and can rescue you from dangerous places.

Use pages 38-39 to work on memorizing Psalm 23.

Take a moment and write Psalm 23 in your own words. Focus on the truth of the Scripture, and be confident that God walks with you as you submit your life to His lordship.

> Praise God for His presence. Let the words to this psalm, a favorite praise song, or hymn guide the words of your prayer.

day 16

MENDING A BROKEN HEART

discover

Have you ever had a broken heart? Have you ever felt crushed inside? No one likes or wants to experience these feelings, but we've probably all felt like this from time to time. We feel this way because we're human—we aren't unbreakable physically or emotionally. People say mean things. We experience rejection. Thankfully, there is good news. There is hope for the brokenhearted.

READ PSALM 34.

The LORD is near the brokenhearted; he saves those crushed in spirit.
—Psalm 34:18

David wrote this psalm during one of the most crushing seasons in his life. He was on the run from King Saul because God had chosen David to be the new King of Israel instead of Saul. Saul wasn't very interested in giving up his throne, so he wanted to kill David. David fled to a place called Gath. When he arrived, to protect himself from danger, he pretended to be insane.

But look at the words David wrote in response to this experience: "I will bless the LORD" (v. 1), "boast in the LORD" (v. 2), and "proclaim the LORD's greatness" (v. 3). How could a man whose only choice to survive was faking insanity say such things? David's relationship with God ran deeper than his fear and feelings. He *knew* God was near, even when he felt brokenhearted and crushed.

delight |

As a verb, the word *delight* means to please someone greatly. As a noun it means great pleasure.[6]

How do you take delight in the Lord when you feel brokenhearted and crushed?

How can you bring delight to the Lord, even when you feel brokenhearted and crushed?

> **Ask God to help you know in your heart that He is good and He is near when you are heartbroken. Use Psalm 34 as a prayer. If you find that parts of it are difficult to pray, turn David's proclamation of faith into a request for deeper trust in the Lord's goodness.**

display |

We know that we'll face heartbreak in life. Having an idea of how you'll approach difficult days might help you walk through them without sliding into despair.

Write: *God is close to the brokenhearted. Therefore I will...* Then write out five things you plan to do the next time you experience heartbreak.

If you are feeling down today, then write out Psalm 34:18 on a piece of paper. Fold that paper and put it in your pocket. Whenever you feel sadness creeping in, take out the paper, read it, and be reminded that the Lord is closer than you can imagine.

day 17

JUST BE THERE

discover

If someone asked you what a fish looks like, you probably wouldn't have any difficulty answering that question. A fish lives in water, has fins and gills, eyes on the sides of its head, and can be a variety of colors. But when someone asks what a Christian looks like, the answer might not come so easily. Thankfully, several places in the Bible describe what it looks like to be a Christian.

READ
ROMANS 12:9-16.

Rejoice with those who rejoice; weep with those who weep.
—*Romans 12:15*

This list is full of instructions for what to do and what not to do as Christ followers. The character traits on this list should be words that people would use to describe us.

Christians should "Rejoice in hope; be patient in affliction; be persistent in prayer" (v. 12). But he also said to take time to weep with those who weep. God calls us to be empathetic people—attempting to understand how others feel. God calls us to pause and care for others. God calls us to listen to those who are hurting. God calls us to be there for those who are struggling to find joy.

delight |

We can become empathetic people. We can try to think about how we would feel in their situation. We can try to be good friends. Sometimes, just being there and listening is the best thing you can do.

An important verse to remember to help us be empathetic is the shortest verse in the Bible: "Jesus wept" (John 11:35). Jesus was human just like us. He felt pain and sorrow with and for others. We are called to do the same. What do you need to do in your own heart to be more available to weep with others?

> **It's not always easy to be there for others. Pray that God would move in your heart to make you more empathetic. Ask Him to give you opportunities to simply be there for someone else.**

display |

Sometimes people stay stuck in depression because no one bothers to reach out to them and weep with them. No one is there for them.

Have you taken time out of your life to just pause and listen to someone? If you haven't lately, here's a challenge for you. Text a friend you know who might be hurting. Arrange a time to sit down with them and just talk. When you get there, put away your phone or anything that might distract you, look them in the eye, and just listen.

day 18

WEAKNESS > STRENGTH

discover

Time and again, God's Word reveals that God is near the brokenhearted and calls us to be there for those who are struggling. But God could be working through depression in ways we never imagined.

READ
2 CORINTHIANS 12:1-10.

But he said to me, "My grace is sufficient for you, for my power is perfected in weakness." Therefore, I will most gladly boast all the more about my weaknesses, so that Christ's power may reside in me. So I take pleasure in weaknesses, insults, hardships, persecutions, and in difficulties, for the sake of Christ. For when I am weak, then I am strong. —2 Corinthians 12:9-10

God used the Apostle Paul to do great things. During his ministry, Paul planted churches, wrote much of the New Testament, and shared the gospel with too many people to count. If anyone would be perceived as strong, it would be Paul. But in these verses, Paul was bragging about his weaknesses. Why would he do that? Because when we know we can't do something on our own, we're more likely to ask for help.

God gave Paul a built in weakness (v. 7) so that he would rely on the Lord. God can use even depression as an opportunity for us to lean more closely into Him. When you struggle, when you feel like you can't take another step, pause and think of how God might be working through you in this situation.

delight

Let's be clear: God doesn't want us to be depressed, and He doesn't give us depression. We need to know God is so big and mighty that He can use something bad, like depression, for good in the long run. But we have to view it through a certain lens.

Read Romans 8:28. How can God use the negative and discouraging things in life—things like depression—for His glory and our good?

Read Psalm 30:11. What has to happen in your life for you to be able to joyfully proclaim these verses from your own heart?

display

One of the ways God turns our weakness into His strength is by giving us opportunities to use our experiences to speak truth and hope into others' lives.

What have you endured that you might be able to share with others to help them walk through difficult days?

Who walked with you through your difficult days? Name one person who was there for you. Consider texting that person today to tell them thank you.

> **Ask God to help you see how what you've been through might help someone else. Then, thank God for that person (or people) who walked with you through your trial.**

resources

books
- *Unshakable Hope* by Max Lucado
- *What to Do When You Don't Know What to Do: Discouragement and Depression* by Henry Cloud and John Townsend
- *Healing Depression for Life* by Dr. Gregory Jantz
- *Encouragement for the Depressed* by Charles H. Spurgeon

articles
- "Why Christian Love Matters in Depression" by Kathryn Butler (The Gospel Coalition, 2018)
- "8 ways to help depressed Christians" by David Murray (The Ethics and Religious Liberty Commission [ERLC], 2017)
- "How the church can be a community to those with depression" by Garrick D. Conner (ERLC, 2019)

videos
- "God Wants to Lift You out of Depression" by Tony Evans (Youtube)
- "How Should We Respond to Suffering? | Kelly Minter" by LifeWay Christian Resources (Youtube)
- "How does the gospel speak hope in the battle with depression?" by Jennifer Michelle Greenburg (ERLC)

find a counselor

Always, always talk with your parents if you're struggling. If you want to talk to a counselor or if your parents have approached you about doing so, these tools can help.

This list is certainly not exhaustive, but you and your parents can do the following to help you find a solid, biblical counselor.

- Check with your church first to see if they have qualified counselors on-site or have a list of recommended counselors to refer you to.
- Use a reputable search site to find a Christian Counselor near you. These sites provide a search-by-location feature, but it's still a good idea to go through your results and make sure the counselor has experience with depression. These two sites are good places to start.
    - The Christian Counselor's Network (powered by Focus on the Family)
    - Christian Care Connect (powered by the American Association of Christian Counselors)

in case of emergency

Sometimes depression roots itself deep inside and causes suicidal thoughts. If you're experiencing any of these thoughts, please reach out now. Even if you aren't experiencing these thoughts, you may know someone who is. Here are some people you can contact if you need help.

- If you have a counselor, contact them immediately. Most counselors have an emergency line for off-hours.
- National Suicide Prevention Lifeline. Call 1-800-273-8255 or chat on their website at https://suicidepreventionlifeline.org.
- New Hope Telephone Counseling Center. Call 714-639-4673 to connect with a trained crisis prevention specialist.
- National Alliance on Mental Illness. Call 1-800-950-6264.
- To Write Love on Her Arms. Text TWLOHA to 741741 for their crises text line, and check out their resources page here: https://twloha.com/find-help/. On this page you'll find links to 24-hour hotlines and other helps.

day 19

DWELL

discover

When we talk about Scripture and faith as part of overcoming depression, this doesn't discount the fact that we might need medication and counseling too. God created each one of us uniquely, and He also provides various tools to help us overcome depression. But Scripture is key because it draws us closer to God, changing us and the way we think. Our mindset about joy is an important and necessary element in overcoming despair in our lives. It helps us to manage, and at times overcome, depression.

READ
PHILIPPIANS 4:4-8.

Finally brothers and sisters, whatever is true, whatever is honorable, whatever is just, whatever is pure, whatever is lovely, whatever is commendable— if there is any moral excellence and if there is anything praiseworthy— dwell on these things. —Philippians 4:8

Have you ever wanted something so much that it dominated your thoughts? You start seeing this thing you want everywhere you look, and you notice other people who have it. This is what it means to dwell on something.

In today's passage, the Apostle Paul instructed us to dwell on certain things—things that bring joy. To simply believe that these things are good doesn't get you where you need to be. If we want to have joy in our lives and fight against depression, then we have to dwell on good things.

delight |

When Paul instructed us to "rejoice in the Lord" (v. 4), he wrote from a prison cell. He knew what it was like to live through difficult days, and still he rejoiced.

Think about the list Paul wrote in verse 8. Which people in your life mirror these qualities? List one beside each of the following.

- Truthfulness:
- Honor:
- Justice:
- Purity:
- Loveliness:
- Being commendable (admirable):
- Moral Excellence:

display |

Ask yourself these questions to help you consider how you might display to others that you're focusing on joyful things.

Are my words joyful? Which words need to be added and deleted from my vocabulary to bring more joy to my life?

Are my actions joyful? Which actions need to be added and deleted from my daily activities to bring more joy to my days?

> **It takes real effort to focus on joyful things. Spend some time talking to God about where your mind usually wanders. Ask Him to direct your thoughts and help you dwell on Him and things that are good.**

day 20

NEVER ALONE

discover

On a TV show called *Alone*, survival experts are dropped in remote places, and they try to live with only a few survival tools all by themselves. The winners often stay weeks in hostile places, talking to themselves and eating gross things (like squirrels and bugs) just to survive. That sounds terrifying, right?

For a moment, Joshua thought he would be alone. Technically, he would never be by himself like the people on *Alone*, but he would be without his leader. For years, Moses led the Hebrews—from slavery in Egypt to freedom and the edge of the promised land. His time as leader was ending and Joshua would be taking over.

READ
DEUTERONOMY 31:1-8.

"The LORD is the one who will go before you. He will be with you; he will not leave you or abandon you. Do not be afraid or discouraged." —Deuteronomy 31:8

Even though Joshua wouldn't have Moses as they crossed the Jordan River and entered the promised land, he had someone better. God would not just go with Joshua, He would go before him. God would be the One who would take care of the people. God would be the One who would drive out their enemies. By no means would Joshua be alone; the Lord Almighty was with him.

> **Take a moment and reflect on this truth. God is with you. He goes before you. Thank Him for doing this. Write out specific moments when you could feel His presence with you.**

LifeWay Students | Devotions

delight |

We know God is with us, but sometimes we still feel alone. Have you ever felt this way? Why or why not?

How has God proven to you over the course of your life that you are not alone?

How has God "gone before you"?

display |

Think about your friends. Who might feel alone? List any names that come to mind. Consider a way you can connect with them more deeply, write it beside their name, and act on it.

When you're tempted to tell yourself that you're alone, try speaking aloud the words: *God goes before me, I am never alone.*

day 21

REMEMBER

discover

You may not be familiar with Habakkuk. He was an Old Testament prophet who lived about 600 years before Jesus was born. During his lifetime, the Jewish people were under siege from the Babylonians. Eventually, they would fall to Babylon and be forcefully removed from Jerusalem. Imagine being taken from your home and forced to live in another country.

READ
HABAKKUK 3:16-19.

Though the fig tree does not bud and there is no fruit on the vines, though the olive crop fails and the fields produce no food, though the flocks disappear from the pen and there are no herds in the stalls, yet I will celebrate in the LORD; I will rejoice in the God of my salvation!
—Habakkuk 3:17-18

There's no way to disguise it. Life for the Jews was awful during these years. Habakkuk depicted their reality by comparing their situation to trees that didn't bloom, fields that didn't yield crops, and animals who disappeared from their pastures. In spite of all of this sadness and hardship, Habakkuk still found joy in the Lord because of his salvation.

You might totally identify with Habakkuk. You might feel like nothing is going right for you at the moment. But you can still have joy the same way Habakkuk did—by remembering your salvation.

delight

When did you give your life to Christ? Who was with you? Where were you? How did you feel when you started your faith journey? Consider recording your testimony and sharing it with friends who need to hear the gospel.

If you haven't experienced salvation, talk with your parents, a trusted leader, or your student pastor about what it means to place your faith in Jesus.

Read John 6:47. How can you be assured that you truly have been saved by Christ?

> **Read Romans 8:38-39 aloud as a prayer. With boldness and confidence, praise the Lord that nothing—no matter how bad it may seem—can separate you from His love.**

display

Repetition helps us remember. So, repeat to yourself the end of Habakkuk 3:18 today: "I will rejoice in the God of my salvation!"

Think about your life. Write out one difficult thing you experienced in the past and one difficult thing you're experiencing now. Then, beside each thing, write the phrase, *I will rejoice in the God of my salvation.*

day 22

THE LAST WORD

discover

We need leaders. Without leaders, there's no clear direction for people to follow. No one to come to with questions. No one to teach us the right way. When leaders give commands, it's for our good. Think about someone in your life who's been a great leader, and keep in mind what makes them so awesome.

READ
ISAIAH 41:8-16.

Do not fear, for I am with you; do not be afraid, for I am your God.
I will strengthen you; I will help you;
I will hold on to you with my righteous right hand.
—Isaiah 41:10

God is our ultimate leader. Here we see the Lord giving a clear command to His people, "Do not fear, for I am with you." When God said these things, His people were in a difficult situation. Because of their disobedience, they were on the verge of being conquered by Babylon.

They had slipped away from God, but they were still His people, and He dearly loved them. They would have to face the results of their sin, but their sin wouldn't have the last word.

God, our leader, gave His people an order: "Do not be afraid, for I am with you." He says the same thing to us. We just have to believe it.

LifeWay Students | Devotions

> **Are there places in your life where you know your actions or words have caused your trouble? If so, ask the Lord to help you turn away from those things. When we live in those sins, it's often more difficult to remember God is with us.**

delight |

There are times in our lives when, like Israel, we cause our own distress. That doesn't mean God is finished with us. He is still there, showing us the way.

It's impossible to experience God's joy while living in sin. In what areas of your life are you holding onto sin while also reaching for God's joy?

It's also important to remember that when we do sin, God doesn't discard us forever. If you are dealing with the aftermath of your sin, take a minute to ask God to help you handle it with grace, but to learn what you can from it so that you can move forward in joy.

display |

Israel's rejection of the Lord meant they had to live in exile for a time, but it didn't mean they were no longer His people. God still had a plan for them, which was ultimately fulfilled in Jesus.

Write this phrase on an index card or sticky note: *My sin does not have the last word—God does.* Because God has the final say over us, we can repent and live in faith instead of fear, knowing He is with us.

day 23

WHAT COMES NEXT?

discover

It seems that almost every movie today is written so they can easily create a sequel if it's successful. While it would definitely bring in more money, people like sequels because they want to know what happens to the characters they've grown attached to. They want to know what comes next in the story.

Yesterday we discussed how our sin causes us pain, but that God is still with us and for us. Now, let's take a look at what comes next.

READ
PSALM 30.

For his anger lasts only a moment, but his favor, a lifetime. Weeping may stay overnight, but there is joy in the morning.
—Psalm 30:5

Here's the truth: God hates sin. Sin brought brokenness into His world and into His people—a people He sent His own Son to pay for. But when we repent and turn from our sins, there is joy. The psalmist explained this well by telling us: "his anger lasts only a moment, but his favor, a lifetime" (v. 5).

The poet Alexander Pope coined the phrase, "hope springs eternal."[7] This phrase is exactly what we have in God. Every day our hope is renewed. We may weep for a season, but joy comes in the morning. Every day our hope springs up again.

The "sequel" to the Lord's anger toward our sin is the joy that comes with our repentance and His forgiveness.

delight

At times, we might be tempted to slip into sin because we know God will forgive us. When we do this, we cheapen the sacrifice Jesus made for sin. This is an attitude that does not bring us joy and we should run from it at all costs.

Have you ever felt tempted to fall into sin, knowing God would forgive you? What happened in those situations?

We cheapen God's grace when we willfully disobey Him, knowing His forgiveness awaits us on the other side. How can you avoid this trap?

> **Pray that God will help you avoid the trap of willful disobedience. Ask Him to remind you of the joy He brings and live in that rather than experiencing the pain of sin.**

display

Remember that God is for you, not against you. He wants you to experience joy. There is no joy in sin. Using a dry-erase marker on a mirror, write out: *God wants me to experience joy.*

In verse 4, David instructed his readers to "sing to the Lord." The next step in the sequence after forgiveness is worship. Write your own psalm of praise to God for His forgiveness. It doesn't have to rhyme, it just needs to come from your heart.

day 24

A THIN LINE

discover

Sometimes the space between pain and joy is razor thin. Think about it like this: Have you ever crossed a finish line? If you have, then you know what a rush it can be. But you can't feel that rush without the pain of running the race first. No matter how sore your legs are or how difficult it is to breathe, when you pass through that tape at the end, all of the pain fades away. This reality is a great picture of what Jesus endured on the cross.

READ
HEBREWS 12:1-2.

For the joy that lay before him, he endured the cross, despising the shame, and sat down at the right hand of the throne of God. —Hebrews 12:2b

Jesus never experienced worse pain than the cross. He had the weight of all the world's sins upon Him and the pain of separation from His Father. Yet, He endured the cross because of the joy that came after it. Above all, He looked forward to the joy of pleasing His Father. The joy of making a way for humanity to be saved. The joy of being glorified for eternity in heaven (Rev. 4:8). For Jesus, the joy of doing His Father's will outweighed the pain, so He willingly laid down His own life.

Just like Jesus did, we can endure the pain in life, knowing that eternal joy is on the other side.

> **Thank Jesus for being willing to endure the pain of the cross. Without His willingness to face that pain, we would not have an opportunity to be saved.**

delight |

There will be points in your life where the path to joy leads through pain. When you find yourself here, remember Jesus.

Describe a time in your life when you had to walk through pain before you could experience joy. How did you endure it? What kept you going even though it hurt?

At times, the painful part of our faith journey will come from persecution. Have you ever felt persecution for your faith in Jesus? How did you manage that pain? How did the Holy Spirit help you endure?

Hebrews 12:1 mentioned the "large cloud of witnesses." These are our Christian brothers and sisters who have gone before us. How does it feel to know that they are cheering you on right now from heaven?

display |

Hebrews 12:2 mentioned Jesus being seated at the right hand of God. The place on the right hand side of a king was for a person of highest rank.[8] As believers, Jesus must have the highest ranking place in our lives.

How do you display to others that Jesus is the most important person in your life?

How can you remember Jesus to help you get through tough times?

MEMORY VERSE

Trust in the Lord with all your heart, and do not rely on your own understanding; in all your ways know him,

and he
will make
your paths
straight.

PROVERBS 3:5-6

day 25

A HOPEFUL FUTURE

discover

Joy is attainable but depression is also a real issue. Yes, even people who love Jesus can be depressed. But we can be joyful, even when it's difficult.

READ
JEREMIAH 29:10-14.

"For I know the plans I have for you"—this is the Lord's declaration—"plans for your well-being, not for disaster, to give you a future and a hope."
—Jeremiah 29:11

While you might be familiar with this verse, its context is often overlooked. Jeremiah was writing to the Jews who had just been conquered and deported from their homeland. They were a broken people who had 70 more years of living in another country under the rule of a foreign king. But right in the middle of this scriptural "reality check" is a beautiful declaration of hope.

Essentially, God said, "I know what you're going through, and I have plans for you that are better than you can imagine." Believing this is step one of what we do when being joyful is difficult. We have to remember that God is good. We have to know—regardless of our circumstances—God has a plan for us and His plan is not to bring disaster on us, but to give us a hopeful future.

delight |

Finding joy in whatever circumstances we face requires us to firmly believe in God and His goodness.

Ask yourself: *Do I believe God is good? Do I believe He has a plan for me? Do I believe His aim is for my ultimate good and not disaster?*

How do you reconcile the difficulties of life with the goodness of God?

display |

When it's difficult to feel joyful, Jeremiah says we should pray in addition to believing the goodness of God. But this isn't a half-hearted, routine, or silent prayer; this type of prayer is desperate and comes from our very souls (Rom. 8:26). The Lord said, "you will seek me and find me when you search for me with all your heart" (v. 13).

When it's tough to feel joyful, are you searching for God with all your heart?

> **Dwell on the goodness of God. Write out a prayer of confession. Confess where you've doubted God's goodness. Confess where you've struggled to find joy. Ultimately, confess that you love Him and trust Him. Then, write out one prayer request for someone you know is struggling to trust God's goodness and present it to Him in prayer.**

day 26

SPOILER ALERT

discover

Are you ever tempted to take the book you're reading and go to the final pages just to see how it resolves? Or do you read the episode descriptions for the show you are binging on Netflix, just to get a hint of where the story will end? Most of us have felt this desire before—maybe even acted on it.

Jesus understood this desire and gave His disciples a heads up on what their future would look like. He didn't give them the full story, but told them something about the theme of their future.

READ
JOHN 16:31-33.

"I have told you these things so that in me you may have peace. You will have suffering in this world. Be courageous! I have conquered the world."
—John 16:33

Jesus was just hours away from being arrested, falsely tried, and crucified. He knew the end was near. As He was giving His disciples some final instructions and encouragement, He tried to spell it out very clearly for them, "Guys, I'm going away, but I'll be back." This didn't sink in for His disciples, though. So then Jesus dropped the ultimate spoiler: "be courageous! I have conquered the world" (v. 33).

Here's the thing: Jesus had not gone to the cross yet. He had not been resurrected yet. He had not ascended into heaven yet. But He knew what was coming. So He could say, "I have conquered the world" (v. 33). That same Jesus who had the certainty to say He had conquered the world before His death, burial, resurrection, and ascension, is the same Jesus who is in charge of your life today. When you think about it from that angle, tackling the whole, "Be courageous!" part becomes a lot easier.

delight

When Jesus said He conquered the world, it doesn't mean He took over or defeated the world with military force. It means He won the victory over sin and death (1 Cor. 15:55-57).

How does knowing Jesus conquered sin and death bring you joy?

Jesus also said that we will have suffering in this world (v. 33). How does knowing that He has conquered the world help you have joy in the middle of suffering?

display

When we know how a story will end, sometimes people want us to keep it to ourselves. But that's not the case with the gospel; it's okay to "spoil" the ending to encourage others.

Who can you talk with about the joy you've found in Jesus? When you have this conversation, it's okay to be real. You don't have to sugar-coat anything; instead, you can let them know that following Christ isn't easy, but it brings joy.

> **Ask God to help you know who to share the joy of Jesus with.**

day 27

REST

discover

Sometimes even giants in the faith have moments of despair. In Matthew 11, we see one such instance: John the Baptist. This is the man Jesus described by saying, "among those born of women no one greater than John the Baptist has appeared" (Matt. 11:11). But a few verses earlier, as John sat in a prison cell, he had a moment of doubt. He asked his followers to go verify with Jesus that He really was the Messiah. Jesus didn't scold them. Instead, He scolded those who didn't believe John's message of preparation for the Messiah. (See Luke 7:18-23.)

READ
MATTHEW 11:28-30.

"Come to me, all of you who are weary and burdened, and I will give you rest. Take up my yoke and learn from me, because I am lowly and humble in heart, and you will find rest for your souls. For my yoke is easy and my burden is light."

When we don't feel like being joyful, we sometimes play this little game in our heads that God is mad at us for having doubts. The enemy then uses that to try to put distance between us and God. But look again at what Jesus said: "Come to me." He did not say, "come to me only if you have no doubts" or "come to me only those who have their act together," or even, "come to me those who aren't struggling." He said come to me "all who are weary and burdened." That includes doubters, mess-ups, and strugglers.

No matter where you are, the call to come extends to you.

delight |

Jesus wasn't saying following Him is easy. In fact, He went out of His way in other places to say how difficult it would be (Matt. 10:22). What He was trying to show is that He empathizes with our pain. He knows what it's like to be human, and He is there for us (Heb. 4:15).

How does it affect you to know that you don't have to change anything about yourself before you come to Jesus?

How has the enemy tried to put distance between you and God?

display |

It's true that Jesus calls us just as we are, but He doesn't want us to stay just as we are. He wants us to grow to be more like Him. Take inventory of the past year. Write out three ways you're more like Christ. Then, write out three ways you need to submit yourself more fully to Him.

> **Thank God that Jesus understands our needs, but still allows us to come to Him and find peace and joy.**

day 28

TRUST GOD

discover

It's not unusual for movies and TV shows to portray someone facing a tough decision, asking a wiser person for advice, then being told, "Just trust your heart." When they do, everything usually turns out okay. While this seems like sound advice, it doesn't align with the teachings of Scripture.

READ
PROVERBS 3:1-11.

Trust in the LORD with all your heart, and do not rely on your own understanding; in all your ways know him, and he will make your paths straight.
—Proverbs 3:5-6

According to these verses, trusting your heart is the last thing you should do. Our hearts are flawed (Jer.17:9). Our hearts often tell us to look out for ourselves above all else. Our hearts tell us to run and hide when we're scared. Our hearts—from time to time—whisper to us lies like, "You're a failure" or "You'll never measure up." When we're struggling to find joy, listening to ourselves is usually the last thing we should do.

Instead, we should listen to the wisdom of these verses. We should trust in the Lord wholeheartedly. We should not trust our own understanding. We should know Him and follow His lead. And we should trust that He will guide us down the right path. This advice is the opposite of what the world tells us, but it is the path into joy and out of despair.

> Think about the path of your life. Where you've been obedient to follow His path, thank Him for His direction. Where have you chosen to try your own way? Ask for forgiveness in those areas.

delight |

When have you taken a wrong path because you trusted your heart? Has the Lord redeemed that mistake in your life? If so, how?

What are some ways you can grow in your knowledge of God and travel down the straight paths He has for you?

display |

There are many ways to grow in your relationship with God, and one of the best ways is Scripture memory.

Re-write Proverbs 3:5-6 in your own words.

Use pages 62-63 to guide you as you try to memorize these verses.

Practice leaning on the Lord to lead you on right paths by pausing to pray before making an important decision. If God leads you to choose something other than what you wanted, ask Him to help you find joy in it and to believe that He has your best interest in mind.

day 29

SEEING JESUS

discover

One of the greatest comforts we have when other believers die is knowing that we will see them again. We know that their life isn't over; in fact it's just beginning. Imagining them with Jesus is often the thought that sustains Christians through our grief.

READ
JOHN 16:19-22.

"So you also have sorrow now. But I will see you again. Your hearts will rejoice, and no one will take away your joy from you." —John 16:22

Jesus knew He was about to be leaving the disciples, first through His death, then again after His resurrection through His ascension back into heaven. He knew that His crucifixion would seem like the end of the world for His followers, but would seem like a great victory for those who opposed Him. He knew He would return from the grave. He knew no one could take away the joy His disciples would feel.

This reality is the same for us two thousand years later. Jesus has risen, and He is coming again. On that day, we will finally see Him. This knowledge has to sustain us on the days when joy is tough. We have to know that this is not the final stop on our journey.

Of course we want our time on Earth to be great, but on the days when it's not, we must believe better days are ahead. We have this hope because we know Jesus will return one day. On that day, all sorrow, pain, and suffering will come to an end (Rev. 21:3-8).

delight |

Unlike the disciples, we've never seen Jesus with our own eyes, but we believe in Him.

What sustains your belief in Jesus, even though you've never seen Him?

How does knowing that He will return help sustain joy in your life, even when it's tough to be joyful?

> **Talk honestly with the Lord about where you are today. Do you lack joy, or are you full of joy? Ask Him to remind you that He will return and one day make all things new.**

display |

The hardest part of waiting is not knowing when Jesus will return and make all things new.

Write out two ways that you will strive to live in joy, knowing Jesus will return and we will see Him.

The joy we'll have when Jesus returns will be everlasting. Write out one sentence expressing how much you are looking forward to that day. Seek out someone to share this joy with today.

day 30

ALWAYS

discover

There will always be tough days, discouraging moments, and maybe even seasons of depression. But God has given us tools to help us find joy no matter what we're facing. Most of all, Jesus has made a promise to us that can sustain us even on the darkest of days.

READ
MATTHEW 28.

"And remember, I am with you always, to the end of the age."
—Matthew 28:20b

There are two promises in this chapter that can sustain us as we seek joy in our lives.

Jesus is alive. The angel at Jesus' empty tomb told the ladies not to be afraid (v. 5). But it's not enough just to try to not be afraid, we need to know why we shouldn't fear. The angel gives the reason in verse 6: Jesus has risen from the grave. We don't have to be afraid anymore because Jesus is alive.

Jesus is with us. No matter what we go through, how challenging things may be, how dark life appears to be: Jesus is always with us. Because Jesus is alive and with us, we can walk with confidence through our days.

Our joy in life comes entirely from these two truths. Without them there is no joy. Because these two things are true, we have life, hope, and joy—inexpressible and unattainable for those who do not know Christ. And we won't want to keep this news to ourselves.

> **Spend a few minutes thanking God for Jesus. Thank Him for the resurrection, and thank Jesus for His continued presence in your life.**

delight

How can focusing on Jesus' resurrection relieve your fears?

How does knowing that Jesus is alive and with you give you confidence to face whatever lies before you?

display

Spending time in the Bible or doing a devotion on joy doesn't mean you'll always be really joyful. But it will show you the way God's Word defines true joy, along with how to seek it, sustain it, and share it with others.

List three key takeaways from studying joy.

What one thing about joy can you share with someone else that might help them have more joy?

JOY IN THESE PAGES
How faith heroes handled despair.

Traditionally in the church, Christians have often felt like it was wrong for them to feel down or struggle with seasons of depression. Today, we understand that depression is the result of a fallen world—and while it may result from personal sin, this isn't always the case. As with all of life's biggest questions, we turn to our ultimate source of truth—God's Word—for the answer.

The Bible doesn't diagnose any of our faith heroes with depression as a consistent mental health issue. But we do know that countless biblical characters experienced moments or seasons of darkness and despair—including Jesus Himself. By studying their lives on the pages of Scripture, we can learn how to fight depression from a spiritual perspective. We can experience true and lasting joy.

ELIJAH
Read 1 Kings 19.

After God's powerful display with the prophets of Baal, Jezebel threatened Elijah, and He ran in fear. Once he reached the wilderness, he cried out to God: "I have had enough! Lord, take my life" (1 Kings 19:4). Elijah felt alone and afraid; He was so distraught that he wished for death. God responded by first taking care of Elijah's needs for food and rest, then God gave Elijah the gift of His presence on the mountain (vv. 11-12). Only then did God send Elijah forward to anoint Elisha to be his help and successor.

DAVID
Read Psalm 13:1-6; 55:4-5; 69:1-36.

If you look at the Davidic Psalms, it won't take long to see that David experienced countless victories and days of despair. He went from hiding from a king bent on killing him, to becoming king himself, to having an affair and committing murder, to repentance and restoration. With David, it's important to note that moments of his despair were related to his own sin, so his response to that was rightly his repentance (Ps. 51:1-19). But when the circumstances were beyond His control, he still cried out to God: "How long, Lord? Will you forget me forever? … How long will I store up anxious concerns within me, agony in my mind every day?" (Ps. 13:1-2). Interestingly, even when David began a Psalm with despair, he typically ended in praise, affirming his trust in God (Ps. 13:5-6).

JOB
Read Job 1-3, focusing on 3:1-7,11-12; 42:1-17.

Job's life was turned upside down—he lost everything he owned, along with livestock, servants, and even children. The Bible calls his suffering "very intense" (Job 2:13). His friends assumed it was the result of sin, and his wife told him to curse God and die. But Job said no. While Job remained faithful to God in every trial, he also "cursed the day he was born" (Job 3:1). God allowed Job to suffer before He stepped in, but God didn't leave Job alone in this time of tragedy. God reminded Job of who He was. Job's response is one we should strive to imitate in times of despair: "I know that you can do anything and no plan of yours can be thwarted. … I reject my words and am sorry for them" (Job 42:2,6). He humbly recognized what God spoke through the prophet Isaiah: "my ways are higher than your ways, and my thoughts than your thoughts" (Isa. 55:9). Then God restored Job's possessions, gave him more children, and blessed Him immensely (Job 42:10,12).

JEREMIAH
Read Jeremiah 15:10-11 and Lamentations 3:14-20,22-26.

Aside from the fact that Jeremiah wrote an entire book titled Lamentations (a lament is a passionate expression of grief or sorrow), he actually said he had "become depressed" (Lam. 3:20). Jeremiah was alone and rejected, and people even planned to harm him. He cried out to God many times throughout his ministry, even angrily asking why his pain was "unending" (Jer. 15:18). God responded to Jeremiah, asking him to repent of his anger, while also assuring Jeremiah that he would be safe (Jer. 15:19-21). Jeremiah responded by asking God for healing (Jer. 17:14). Much like David, Jeremiah often expressed his troubled heart to the Lord, then returned to praise (Lam. 3:20-26).

JESUS
Read Isaiah 53:3-5; Hebrews 4:15; and Luke 22:40-46.

Before you declare this statement heretical, this is not a claim that Jesus was depressed—far from it. Rather, this is a claim that Jesus experienced deep sadness, just like we do (Isa. 53:3; Heb. 4:12). Just before He was arrested, He cried out to His Father, asking if there was another way. He prayed so fervently that "his sweat became like drops of blood"(Luke 22:44). As He became sin on the cross, He cried out to His Father in despair, "My God, my God, why have you abandoned me" (Matt. 27:46). The way Jesus responded to His suffering teaches us about our greatest weapons for fighting darkness.

Delight

WHAT WE CAN LEARN

Though these are only short summaries of the lives of these Bible heroes, we can learn the key to driving the darkness of depression right out of our lives. Every single one of these people cried out to God for help—or in repentance if necessary—then they continued walking the path God had called them to. Let's take a look at some specific ways we can imitate their example when we face seasons of despair.

Acknowledge God. Like Job, recognize that as God, the Father has the right to give or take whatever He wants (1:21); that He can do anything and His plans will always move forward (Job 42:2). We can also submit to His authority and say, "not my will, but yours, be done" like Jesus did (Luke 22:42).

Pray. When life gets you down cry out to God. Tell Him exactly how you're struggling. Elijah told God that he wanted to die. David asked God to answer him and be compassionate (Ps. 69:16). Job said he'd asked for help and God didn't answer (30:20). Jeremiah expressed his anger, saying he felt like God was "a mirage" (15:18). And Jesus asked, "if you are willing, take this cup away from me" (Luke 22:42). While we should always approach God with the reverence He deserves, we can open our hearts to Him. He's the only One who can truly bring light and healing.

Praise. It's common practice to praise God when He brings us out of a season of despair, but what people like David show is how to praise (delight in) Him even when we feel down. Though David occasionally asked things like where God was or for God to save him from his enemies, he circled back to praise God for who He is. And if we look at Jeremiah, just two verses after saying he was depressed, he affirmed that God's "mercies never end" (Lam. 3:22).

Surround yourself with people who care. We know that the first step is taking our cares to God, but it also helps to talk with compassionate others. You need to find people who will carry your burdens with you. God provided Elisha to help Elijah, and to eventually take over Elijah's ministry. Job's friends—although they gave bad advice—did give him their presence. Jesus shared His heart with His disciples, asking them to pray for Him. We can see the negative effects of not having these people in the fact that Jeremiah had no family or friends, and he is often called "the weeping prophet."

Keep doing the work God has called you to do. Elijah continued to prophesy. David continued to seek God and lead His people. Job continued to believe God and serve him in faithfulness. Jeremiah continued to call God's people to repentance and trusted God to take care of Him. Jesus went to the cross, becoming our sin, dying to pay the price for it, and was resurrected.

REFLECT

What's the greatest truth you've seen from studying the lives of these characters of faith? How will you allow it to influence the way you respond to feeling down in the future?

A PRAYER FOR HELP IN SUFFERING

If you're experiencing a season of darkness, take a minute to sit in God's presence and talk to Him. If you don't know where to start, remember that the Holy Spirit has words to pray for us when we have nothing left to give (Rom. 8:26-27). You can also use the prompt below to help you get started.

God, I recognize that You are God, that You are good and work all things for good for those who love You. I realize that when I respond in godly ways to my suffering, all of the praise and glory goes to You. Thank You for the ways You love, provide for, teach, and hear me. Help me to see You in every aspect of my day. Show me how to take my eyes off of my circumstances and shift my focus to where it belongs—on You. Help me to fully delight in You.

sources

1. Michael Jordan, Forbes Quotes: Thoughts on The Business of Life (Forbes), accessed September 4, 2020, https://www.forbes.com/quotes/11194/.
2. Edwin A. Blum and Trevin Wax, *CSB Study Bible* (Nashville, TN: Holman Bible Publishers, 2017), accessed via mywsb.com.
3. A.W. Geiger and Leslie Davis, "A Growing Number of American Teenagers – Particularly Girls – Are Facing Depression," Pew Research Center (Pew Research Center, May 30, 2020), https://www.pewresearch.org/fact-tank/2019/07/12/a-growing-number-of-american-teenagers-particularly-girls-are-facing-depression/.
4. "G4727 - Stenazō - Strong's Greek Lexicon (KJV)," Blue Letter Bible, accessed September 4, 2020, https://www.blueletterbible.org/lang/lexicon/lexicon.cfm?Strongs=G4727.
5. Adapted from Kessler Psychological Distress Scale (K10)," accessed September 18, 2020, http://www.aci.health.nsw.gov.au/__data/assets/pdf_file/0015/212901/Kessler_10_and_scoring.pdf; Ivan Goldberg, "Depression Test - Do You Have Depression?" Psychology Tests & Quizzes, accessed August 31, 2020, https://psychcentral.com/quizzes/depressionquiz/.
6. "Delight," Merriam-Webster (Merriam-Webster), accessed September 4, 2020, https://www.merriam-webster.com/dictionary/delight.
7. Alexander Pope, *An Essay on Man* (United Kingdom: A. Millar, and J. and R. Tonson, 1767), 10.
8. "What Is the Significance of the Right Hand of God?," accessed September 9, 2020, https://www.compellingtruth.org/right-hand-of-God.html.